T0193246

A TOWN CALLED SOMETIMES

A TOWN CALLED SOMETIMES

Robert Fischer

A TOWN CALLED SOMETIMES

iUniverse books may be ordered through booksellers or by contacting:

iUniverse
1663 Liberty Drive
Bloomington, IN 47403
www.iuniverse.com
1-800-Authors (1-800-288-4677)

Because of the dynamic nature of the Internet, any web addresses or links contained in this book may have changed since publication and may no longer be valid. The views expressed in this work are solely those of the author and do not necessarily reflect the views of the publisher, and the publisher hereby disclaims any responsibility for them.

Any people depicted in stock imagery provided by Getty Images are models, and such images are being used for illustrative purposes only. Certain stock imagery © Getty Images.

ISBN: 978-1-5320-8848-3 (sc)
ISBN: 978-1-5320-8697-7 (e)

Print information available on the last page.

iUniverse rev. date: 11/14/2019

*This Book Is Dedicated To All My Friends And Family
Who Encouraged And Assisted Me In
Its Production. A Special Thanks To My Daughter Anna
Barrera Who Did The Cover And
Other Illustrations For Me.*

CHAPTER 1
Territory of New Mexico-1852

He felt the pain and heard his father's voice at almost the same instant. "Get out of bed you lazy son of a bitch. There's work to do. Do you expect the others to do your work for you?" yelled his father. Armando Reyes jumped out of bed and said, "Damn pa, you didn't have to kick me. I was up most of the night with mama." His mother was in terrible health and was dying of tuberculosis. She was confined to her bed and could no longer do anything that a mother would normally do. Since Armando was the oldest, most of her responsibilities had fallen to him. He didn't really mind the added burden, but his father was cruel and lazy, making everything much more difficult. His father didn't work and spent most of his time at home complaining about how badly life was treating him.

Armando's father and mother didn't sleep in the same bedroom any longer. She had a lot of coughing spells and that would wake up his father who didn't like being disturbed.

Except for the inconvenience, his father really didn't seem to care that his wife was dying.

Armando, now seventeen years old, was lean and about five foot seven inches tall. As a result of all his hard labors, he was very strong and agile. His father had threatened to kill him more than once because he was the only one who dared to stand up to him, but his father was actually afraid of him because he knew Armando always carried a knife and wasn't afraid to use it. It was the boy's only possession and he always had it with him. A rancher had given it to *him* for some work he had done on *his* place. It had an eight inch blade with an inscription on it in Spanish. It read, "Si esta vibora te pica no hay remedio de botica." Roughly translated it meant, "For the bite of this snake there is no remedy."

He, along with his parents and their other six children, lived on a small farm in the southeastern part of the territory of New Mexico and not too far from El Paso. The farm was only about forty five acres, but it had a nice garden and enough grass to support a few cows and horses. Of course, there were other small animals on the place as well. A few chickens, ducks and goats. They always had plenty of milk and eggs and fresh vegetables when they were in season. They grew corn and beans mostly and that provided them with tortillas and frijoles, which made up most of their meals. There was a water well near the house and a small creek about two hundred yards away. There was a nice barn and several smaller out buildings. They had to keep the small animals in a fenced area to keep them safe from predators such as wolves and coyotes. Even big cats were seen in the area occasionally.

Life was not easy for any of the children. They all had assigned chores that they were expected to do every day. Armando had three sisters and three brothers. The girls did all the cooking and cleaning. They washed clothes, did some sewing and helped with gardening. The boys did most of the outside work. Planting and working in the garden, feeding the livestock, milking the cows, gathering the eggs, fetching water for the home and making sure there was plenty of fire wood for cooking and heating. In addition, they would also hunt and fish for a variation in their diet. For income, all of the children would hire out as laborers on adjacent farms or ranches when work was available.

Armando's brothers and sisters never called him by his name. He was always addressed as big brother. When there was a problem, they always came to him. It didn't do any good to talk to their father, as he was not concerned with their well being at all. The only time he showed any interest in them was when he thought they might be able to work and bring home some money.

Armando's mother loved her children and even though she knew she was dying, she maintained a strong religious faith. Every night before retiring she gathered all the children in a circle around her bed. They all held hands while the mother said a prayer for their safekeeping. She prayed for each one of them by name and even prayed for her worthless husband. Her faith never wavered even though she suffered greatly towards the end of her life.

Her six year old daughter disappeared one day and was gone for several hours. Everyone was frantically searching for her except the father. As usual, he was resting and didn't want to be disturbed. Armando and the other children looked everywhere. They checked the house and all the out buildings several times. They looked in the well, fearing she may have fallen into it. They looked in the creek and thoroughly searched all the property. She had simply vanished. The mother was hysterical and in tears. They all thought she had been kidnapped by Indians. Then, just before dark, the little girl walked into the house as if nothing had happened. She had a pretty little bouquet of flowers for her mother, who called her into the bedroom and asked her where she had been. She told her she had spent some time visiting with an angel. They had a wonderful time together gathering flowers in a pretty garden.

The angel was very beautiful and told her she would return in a few days to take her to heaven with her. The angel told her not to be afraid because she would like it there in heaven and would be very happy there.

No one understood what the little girl was talking about.

They assumed she had fallen asleep somewhere out of sight and must have dreamed all this. Three days later, without any warning and showing no symptoms of illness, the little girl died. She looked as though she had simply fallen asleep and her face had a glow or aura of complete peace. This was a sad time for all of them but the mother told them not to feel too badly. The little girl was in heaven now and would never know hunger or pain again.

As the mother grew more ill, life for all of them was more difficult, especially for Armando. He tended to all her needs, day and night. The father got more difficult with time and eventually was hated by all the children. They suffered from constant abuse, both mental and physical. He was never satisfied with anything they did and accused them of being lazy and worthless.

Armando knew his mother was dying. In the final days of his mother's life, he learned that his father was sexually abusing the oldest girl who was only fourteen years of age.

In less than a week the mother died. They buried her next to the little girl and all the children gathered around the gravesite for a simple and final group prayer. They held hands and one of the girls read the Lord's prayer from the mother's bible. After the prayer Armando, or big brother as the siblings called him, told them he knew what was going on with the oldest girl and her father. He knew the others were unhappy also, but now that their mother was gone, he would make things right.

He told the others that he would have to leave home very soon and when he did, his fifteen year old brother would be in charge. They were to obey him and treat him like a father they never had. He told them that he knew they were confused now, but it would all make sense to them the following day.

The next morning, big brother and the father were both gone and there were three graves now, where before there were only two. The snake had struck and there was no cure.

Armando Reyes left home filled with a lot of resentment and a lot of hate.

CHAPTER 2
Comanchero

S omewhere in the territory of New Mexico two rivers ran together. In the fork or V formed by the rivers was a campsite for a small band of Comanche Indians. To the north of the campsite was a large bluff, which created a windbreak and shelter against north winds. The terrain below the bluff was level for a few hundred feet and then dropped again gradually to the largest river, which ran west to east. The smaller river, running southeast and feeding the larger one, formed the eastern boundary for the camp. There were several nearby springs that provided fresh drinking water. This was just one of many sites used by the Indians who moved up and down the rivers when game became scarce in the immediate area.

The Indians, who were all excellent horseman, lived mostly off the game brought in by the men who did the hunting. The many buffalo in the area provided them with meat, which made up the most important part of their diet. In addition, the buffalo hides provided them with clothing and were used to make their shelters or tepees. Deer and antelope were also plentiful, along with some elk, bears and many smaller animals. In addition, the women would harvest nuts, fruit and berries while gathering firewood to warm their shelters or for cooking. There was always a need for firewood as they kept at least one fire burning 24 hours a day.

Everyone in the band had plenty to do and, in some way, would provide for the general welfare of the group. Even the children had assigned chores and worked with the women a great deal. The young boys were no exception and would have to do many menial tasks until they were skilled enough to hunt. It was in this place where the comanchero, Tom Smolly, would take his wife.

Tom Smolly had been trading with the Comanche Indians for many years. He knew enough of the language and some signing to communicate quite well. He had traded with this band many times and they all knew him by sight. He traded mostly for fine buffalo hides and the Indians would trade for almost anything. Their main interest was horses and they knew their horses well.

Occasionally, he would bring them rifles and ammunition or even whiskey, although authorities frowned upon this.

On one of his visits he saw a young girl who looked to be between 15 to 20 years old. She seemed to be in very good health and was relatively attractive. When he expressed an interest in the girl he was told she had recently lost her husband, who had been gored and killed by a buffalo during a hunt. She had been taken in by her husband's brother and he might be willing to let her go if the price was right. After much talk and some drinking, the two men came to an agreement. Tom Smolly would give him a rifle with ammunition now and return later with six fine horses, at which time he would be allowed to leave with the girl. This was a stiff price to pay, bur Tom was tired of living alone and cooking his own meals. They sealed the transaction with what was left of the whiskey and Tom headed south to his home.

He lived approximately 25 miles from the encampment in a small cabin next to a creek. He had a nice corral to secure his stock and very little else. As soon as he was able to get the horses, he returned to the Comanche camp and told the Indian he was ready to complete the trade. By this time the young buck had decided he had made a bad trade and wanted two more horses. It took another bout of drinking to convince the Indian to let him take the girl. She left without a struggle while her former caretaker slept.

At first, Tom treated the girl well and she served his every need. She did all the cooking and cleaning and most of the work around the cabin. She also went with him on his trading expeditions to care for him during his travels.

Less than a year later she gave birth to a son. When he was a few years old his mother made the comment that the boy was as cunning as a wolf. The name stuck. From that time on he was known only as Wolf. Tom had little use for the boy and abused him greatly. He treated the boy like a slave and when he didn't move quickly enough, he was cuffed, kicked or beaten. The boy could do nothing to Tom's satisfaction and was constantly criticized and ridiculed for being an ignorant Indian. Tom threatened to leave him with the Indians as a slave several times but the boy's mother would not let him.

By the time the boy was able to look after himself, Tom was already tiring of his Comanche wife. He returned her to the same band of Indians and left her there screaming and crying for her son. Tom took the boy back to his cabin and decided the boy was now old enough to do the work of his mother. The boy now had to cook, clean and do any other work that needed to be done. Tom did nothing now but drink and abuse the boy.

Less than 4 days after Tom had left his wife, she was back at the cabin. She told Tom she had come for the boy and wanted to take him back to her home with the Comanche. He laughed and told her she must be crazy or drunk. The boy would stay with him and that was final. She pulled a knife out and attacked Tom, but he grabbed her arm by the wrist and twisted it, making her drop the knife. He then proceeded to strangle her with both hands. She fought back but Tom was too strong. She was starting to lose consciousness when he suddenly relaxed his grip.

Tom had a startled look on his face as he fell backwards, trying to reach the knife planted firmly in his back. When Wolf had seen that Tom intended to kill his mother, he had grabbed the knife from the floor and plunged it deep into his father's back. Tom struggled to get up and free himself of the knife without success. Wolf took Tom's rifle from the wall, pointed it at Tom's chest, and pulled the trigger. The large caliber rifle exploded with a roar putting an end to Tom's misery.

They took everything of value, along with four good horses left in the corral, and returned to her camp. He and his mother had a very tough life with the Comanche but he learned fast and was soon a fine horseman. He went on raiding parties and buffalo hunts. He learned the Comanche tongue and learned sign language as well. In addition, he acted as interpreter when English speaking comancheros or traders came to the village. In this way, he stayed proficient in both languages. He was a true survivalist and could live on whatever nature provided. He had been with the Indians for only 3 years but at the age of 15 he had already proven himself in battle. He owned a fine horse and a Winchester rifle and ammunition.

A few months after his 15th birthday, he decided to strike out on his own. He took all his personal belongings, told his mother goodbye, and headed south. He was, after all, half-white and wanted to explore the white mans way of life.

CHAPTER 3
The Transformation

H is journey took him past the cabin where he and his parents had lived for so many years. He expected to find it rundown and deserted but was surprised to see it was occupied. There were horses in the corral and smoke coming from the chimney. He stayed out of sight and watched the place for several hours. He was sure if they saw him, they would shoot him before he could speak a word. An Indian on the prowl normally meant trouble for any white man.

There were only two men staying in the cabin and appeared to be traders or trappers. He waited until one of the men went to a makeshift outhouse. Wolf was waiting for him as he came out and quietly ended his life with a knife. Eventually, the other man came out to check on his friend and Wolf shot him just as he stepped out the cabin door.

Wolf ransacked the cabin taking some money and anything else of value, including two rifles, a pistol and some supplies. He knew he had to change his appearance if he expected to survive in the white man's world. He took some clothing and tried to dress more like a white man than an Indian. He shortened his hair and bathed in the creek. The transition was not going to be easy but he spoke good English and had the determination to see this thing through.

He spent the night at the cabin. The following morning, he took the best horse in the corral for a pack horse and proceeded south. He followed a faint trail and after a few hours he saw a small cabin with a corral, which held two horses and a milk cow. Again, he watched the place while staying out of sight.

The cabin housed a Mexican family, a man and wife and 3 children. He approached the cabin slowly, leading his horses, and shouting hello to the people inside. The Mexican man stepped outside with a rifle and asked him what he wanted. He told the man he hadn't eaten for several days and had money to pay for a meal. The man invited him in and told him he could join them for a meal already in progress. He hadn't eaten at a real table in quite a while, so he simply observed the others and followed their example.

The man was curious as to what Wolf was doing in the area. He told them he had been doing some hunting and trading with another group of men and grew tired of living in the rough. He was going south to look for work, possibly as a ranch hand. The man told him there was a ranch about a day's ride south. He might want to try there.

Wolf paid the man for the meal and asked if he could rest for a while before leaving. He was told there was no room in the cabin but he was welcome to stay and rest and could find some shelter in the corral. Wolf really wanted to stay and just watch the family and study their ways. All this would help him fit in with other people on his journey into civilization. He remained the entire afternoon and was invited to the evening meal. He again tried to pay for his food but the Mexican would take no more money. He was told he could stay the night but declined, saying he could still travel a few miles before dark.

Wolf rode a couple of hours and stopped for the night.

The following morning, he proceeded south, and in less than a day came to a large ranch. It was almost dark and he thought it would be best to wait until morning before approaching the ranch house.

The following morning, Wolf waited until there was plenty of activity and then rode towards the house. He was stopped by a ranch hand and asked what he wanted. He dismounted, introduced himself as Wolf Smolly, and told the man he was looking for work. The man called for a second man who came out of one of the barns and joined them. The man was introduced as the foreman who again asked Wolf what he wanted. The ranch hand told his boss that Wolf was looking for work. "Are you any good with horses?" asked the man.

Wolf was on his horses back in an instant, immediately brought the horse to a full gallop, stopped and whirled around and brought the horse back at a full run. He rode by the two men dropping down on the side of the horse completely out of their sight. He whirled again and came at the men, again at a full run. Stopping just short of them in a cloud of dust, he leaped from his horse landing on his feet less than a yard from where the two were standing. Wolf was hired on the spot. His job would be to break and train some of the many wild horses on the ranch. If he worked out okay, there would be other work as well.

Wolf was taken to the bunkhouse and shown where he could stay. He was given a tour of the place and introduced to some of the men. After his rounds he was introduced to the owner. The owners name was Hansen. He was a large man and he made it clear he would tolerate no nonsense on his place. As long as Wolf followed orders and did his assigned work, there would be no problems. After the foreman had a chance to see what he could do they would discuss his wages. Hansen took the foreman aside and told him that Wolf's hair looked like it had never been washed, so make sure he showed him the bathhouse.

They wasted no time putting Wolf to work. As soon as he was unpacked and situated in the bunkhouse he was put to work in the corral. It became apparent to the foreman, after just a few hours, that Wolf was an extremely good horseman. By the end of the day the foreman was so impressed he told Wolf he would have work as long as he wanted it, and offered him a good wage. It was late when Wolf had his evening meal and went to the bunkhouse, where he was introduced to the other hands. Wolf didn't have much to say but he watched and listened to the others and was sure he could eventually fit in.

Things went well for a few days. Then one evening in the bunkhouse, one of the men asked him about one of the rifles he had in his possession. It was a special sharps rifle, designed for very long, range accuracy. He explained that he had traded for it up north. The man called him a liar and said he knew the man who had owned that rifle and that he would never have given it up in any kind of a trade. Wolf told him he must be mistaken for he had surely traded for it. The man sneered and said, "Not only are you a liar, but you are stupid to boot." The man pointed out to Wolf some initials on the stock of the rifle. Those are my friend's initials and I say you stole this rifle. Now being called a liar was bad enough, but the man was calling him a thief as well. Wolf responded with some references to the man's mother and said that if there was a liar in the bunch it was the man making all the false charges. With that, the man pulled out a knife and charged at Wolf. A fatal mistake, as Wolf simply stepped to the side, pulled out his own knife and ended the man's life. It was obvious to the other men that Wolf had acted in self- defense but the charges made by the man were serious. If there was an investigation Wolf knew what the results would be.

The following morning he drew his wages, packed his gear and left for Texas. Trouble had a way of finding Wolf, and in a few years, he was wanted by the law in several states.

CHAPTER 4
Mary Elizabeth Orcutt

Mary Elizabeth Orcutt was born to Francis and Matilda Orcutt in 1835 on a large farm in the Territory of New Mexico. The farm was located in what is now known as the Hondo Valley, about 100 miles north of El Paso, Texas. The farm was like an oasis compared to some of the land in that area. It had very rich and fertile soil and plenty of good water.

Her parents were both German and spoke both German and English fluently. Her father was always called Frank and was almost 6 feet tall. He had silver gray hair for as long as Mary could remember and never seemed to tire from his labors on the farm. He was kept busy with maintaining the place and taking care of all the livestock, which consisted of cows, horses, some sheep, all types of poultry and of course, some cats and two dogs.

One dog looked like a large domesticated wolf and roamed the place at will. He was called Chance because there was a good chance, he would kill you if you trespassed on the farm. He was the family security dog and no one came on the place without him knowing it. If a stranger came anywhere near the house they knew immediately not to dismount their horse or wagon until a family member called the dog off. He stayed outside day and night and kept predators away from the livestock.

The second dog, Queeny, was part shepherd and the love of Frank's life. She was no ordinary dog. On command she would bring in the cows for their daily milking. She never made the cattle run but brought them slowly home with an occasional bark at any straggler. Queeny was a natural born sheep dog as well. There was almost nothing she couldn't do with any of the livestock. If the weather looked bad, she would make sure the turkeys and other poultry took shelter in one of the sheds. When it was time to butcher a chicken or two for a meal they would take Queeny to the chicken yard and simply point to the hen they wanted. Queeny would then catch the hen without hurting it and hold it down with her paws until it was retrieved.

She was truly a part of the family and was always let into the house in the evening at supper time. After supper, Frank would take his plate and feed Queeny leftovers. The house they lived in was a large three bedroom home and Mary's bedroom was on one end. At bedtime, Frank would tell Queeny to go with Mary and she would follow her to her room where she slept on the foot of her bed. No matter how cool it might get at night Mary's feet were always warm.

Mary's mother, Matilda, was always called Tillie by Frank and was a very big woman. She was actually a little taller than Frank and weighed over 300 pounds. A very strong woman, Tillie could do the work of any man. She was an excellent cook and proved it every day. Because of all the livestock and Tillie's huge garden the family always ate well.

Of course, everything was prepared on a wood burning cook stove. It was Tillies pride and joy and it was one of Mary's chores to make sure there was a stack of wood next to the stove for cooking.

There was always fresh bread on the table and thanks to all the poultry there were eggs on the table for every meal. That meant boiled or fried eggs for breakfast, lunch or supper. You didn't have to eat them but they were always there.

By the time Mary was 14 she could cook as good as anyone in the valley. The neighbors made a point to never miss an invitation for a meal. There was always plenty and it was always delicious.

Even though Mary loved to spend time with her mother in the kitchen, her first love was working outside with her father. He had never called her Mary. For as long as she could remember, her father had called her Babe. He was an excellent mechanic and even a better carpenter. The house and everything on the farm had been built by him. As a result, Mary had become an excellent carpenter also. She followed Frank around like a puppy and cherished every moment spent with him. Frank and Tillie had no sons and the one other daughter they had, lived only 7 years before she died of pneumonia. Mary was like a son to Frank and he made sure she could work on anything on the farm. All Frank would have to say is let's go Babe and she was at his heel ready to do any work that was necessary.

Frank and Tillie were very kind people and would never turn anyone away who wanted to work or do some chores for a meal. If the person was passing through and needed to spend the night, Frank let them sleep in the barn. But he did have one very strict rule. They had to turn over any tobacco and matches to him before retiring for the night. Frank was terrified of fire as his father and brother had died in a house fire when Frank was a young man. He also knew how long it would take to build another barn. The smokes would be returned in the morning.

Frank was a p1pe smoker himself and Mary would never forget the image of him leaning against the corner of the porch in the evening just before dark, enjoying his pipe. Some evenings all she could make out was his silhouette, in the shadows, with smoke rising over head profiling the thick head of hair and that big German nose. Of course, at his feet lay the ever present Queeny.

There were also the occasional small bands of Indians crossing their land. They were usually looking for food and Frank would let them have a fat lamb, turkey or goose to take with them. He knew if he refused their request for food they would simply return late at night and take what they needed. Because of his kindness to the Indians, they never bothered him and he never lost any other livestock to the Indians.

Mary's parents did not work on Sunday unless it was an emergency. Some of Mary's best memories were the picnics and fishing on pleasant Sunday afternoons. Tillie caught most of the fish and normally Frank didn't fish at all. Instead he built the fire, made the coffee and got everything ready to prepare the fish. As soon as Tillie would start frying the fish the appetizing aroma would fill the air. You could "bet the mortgage" that John Engeldorf, an old neighbor who lived about a half mile away, would show up to have dinner with them. After dinner the men would get out their pipes and tobacco and swap stories. Mary believed that absolutely nothing could taste as good as those fresh fish fried right there on the bank of the river.

Her folks had a spring house that Mary thought was really special too. Frank had built a small building or enclosure over a spring which was about 25 yards from the house. It ran year round and the water was very cold. He had built a trough that ran around the inside of the structure. The water ran around the entire trough and then out through a pipe and forming a stream that provided fresh water for all the livestock. Tillie kept butter and preserves and other things fresh by putting them in closed containers and placing them in the trough of cool water.

Those days on the farm were wonderful but it all came to an end before she reached the age of twenty. Her parents both died of Typhoid Fever leaving her alone to try to run the place. It was too much for Mary and she was just too lonely. There was nothing to keep her there so she sold the place and moved to El Paso. The wonderful memories of the farm slowly faded and she would soon meet a deputy sheriff who would change her life.

CHAPTER 5
El Paso

Mary Orcutt left the farm after her parents death and moved to El Paso early in the year of 1854. She purchased a small home with some of the proceeds from the sale of her parent's farm. She found a good job as a cook in one of the better hotels in town and had a reputation as a marvelous cook.

Mathew Hardin had just gone to work as a deputy sheriff and was celebrating his good fortune over a good meal at that same hotel. It was there that he met Mary and they were immediately attracted to each other. After a very short courtship they married and Mathew, or Matt, as he was called moved in with Mary. They soon had a child and named her Elizabeth. They lived there for six years. Matt worked all that time as a deputy and she worked part time as a cook. Their lives were good and they both liked El Paso.

El Paso was a big, busy and wild town so the jail always had plenty of business. That is where Matt spent most of his time, looking after the jail and the prisoners and trying to keep the place running smooth and quiet. That was quite a chore when the place was full of drunk and rowdy cowboys.

Drunken cowboys were plentiful in El Paso and as a result there were many fights and some shootings. This alone was enough to keep the jail cells full. The jail was normally occupied with drunks sleeping it off and other offenders being held to go before a judge for more serious charges.

Like most of the other deputies, Matt was a big man at 6 foot 5 inches and weighing over 230 pounds. Even though he was a gentle person, he looked pretty menacing with a pistol at his side and a double barreled shotgun cradled in his arms.

Occasionally, he helped out at night when some of the other men made their rounds through the town. He usually went with the sheriff or other deputies if they expected any trouble stopping a brawl or making an arrest. With enough lawmen on hand the rowdies seldom caused any trouble regardless of the situation.

In all the time he had worked as a deputy he was never required to fire either weapon, although it had been necessary to whack a couple of drunks along side the head with the butt of the shotgun. It got their attention every time and after getting up they went along peaceably enough.

Once when assisting in an arrest in one of the saloons, a drunk cowboy was cursing loudly and threatening to shoot all the deputies if they tried to take him in. Matt, who had gotten behind the cowboy, placed the shotgun against the back of his head. At that point, the cowboy seemed to sober quickly and went with them without further outburst.

In addition to his normal duties, Matt had helped deliver some prisoners to Fort Worth, San Antonio and

Austin at different times. The trips had been uneventful but it gave Matt a chance to see the hill country in central Texas. It was so much greener and so much nicer than the flat and mostly dry landscape of West Texas. He fell in love with that part of Texas and planned to visit the area again if the opportunity presented itself

If El Paso was wild, it is impossible for me to give a name to Juarez located just across the Rio Grande in Mexico. In Juarez the bars outnumbered all the other businesses, the ladies outnumbered the men and the drunks filled all the bars. There was plenty of cheap drinks and few lawmen.

When things got to hot for a man in El Paso, he could always seek refuge in Juarez. If he got rough in Juarez he often turned up dead and floating in the Rio Grande. Almost anything was allowed in the bars and all the girls welcomed the Texans and their money. The Mexicans tolerated the gringos as long as the money held out. When that was gone, look out. There were two things not allowed in Juarez. Never touch a real lady on the street and never touch or anger a Mexican lawman. Both could get you in a Juarez jail or dead. Once in a Juarez jail, you might as well be dead for there was little chance of getting out. You could break out or buy your way out if you could get your hands on some money. That was just about your only options. If you stayed out of trouble you could have a hell of a good time in Mexico because the food, drinks and almost all forms of entertainment were really cheap.

On Sunday you could visit the Plaza de Toro's and take in a bullfight and drink beer, if that was a sport you preferred.

The matadors or bullfighters were skilled and the poor bull didn't have much of a chance, but occasionally the bull would turn the tables and send the Matador to the promised land.

Matt and a few deputies had gone to Juarez on more than one occasion but usually avoided the bars as they would likely find themselves drinking next to a Texas fugitive. A bad situation at best, because they were out of their jurisdiction and had no legal rights after crossing the border.

Matt and Mary were both very happy in El Paso. Matt loved his work because it was never boring. Mary took great pride in her little home and enjoyed caring for Elizabeth, or Liz, as they called her. For the most part, they enjoyed a fairly comfortable life style. They had talked about moving to central Texas but Matt had a good paying job and of course, their home was paid for. They would have remained in El Paso but fate would have its say during his sixth year as a deputy.

The sheriff was holding two brothers in the jail for shooting another man in the Fort Worth area. They were to be transferred to Fort Worth in a few days, but would share a cell in the town jail until that time. Neither man seemed very dangerous, but had admitted to the killing saying it was self-defense. As the authorities had it, the two brothers had ambushed the man for a poker stake he had in his possession. The two men had lost all their money in a poker game and thought they had been cheated. They waited outside the saloon for the man to finish his game. They followed him and when the opportunity presented itself, they shot him and relieved him of his winnings. Later, when the brothers were questioned, they denied any wrong doing. They were told to stay in town for a few days until the matter was cleared up, but decided they would be better off in a different location. The brothers were recognized in El Paso and subsequently arrested.

One evening, while at the jail by himself, Matt was taken in by the brothers. One brother fell to the ground and began to yell and scream. He acted as though he was having convulsions and seemed to be in considerable pain. In the excitement, he got too close to the cell and the other brother promptly grabbed him and his pistol. Since he didn't have the keys on him it was a standoff until another deputy returned from his rounds. After the deputy got inside the jail, he was told to bring the keys or Matt would die first and he second. After the second deputy unlocked the cell, his pistol was also taken. The two brothers then took two rifles, but before making their escape, one brother shot both deputies. The brothers escaped into Mexico and avoided the law for many years. They showed up later in a Texas border town where they were arrested by a Texas Ranger and hanged by some vigilantes before they could make it before a judge.

Matt recovered from his wound after several weeks but the other deputy died almost instantly. That was the end of his work as a deputy sheriff in El Paso. Matt blamed the death of the other deputy on his carelessness and no one could convince him otherwise. He knew he wanted a different line of work.

He and Mary decided to sell their home and they went east where they finally bought a small farm south of San

Antonio. They loved the solitude of the country, especially Elizabeth who was now six years old.

Matt was unable to escape the past and soon the word was out that he had been a lawman in El Paso before buying his place on the river. It was also rumored that Matt was the oldest brother of John Wesley Hardin, a notorious murderer who traveled all over Texas trying to evade the law. John Wesley had killed his first man when he was 15 years old and was a fugitive from justice until going to prison in 1878. It was said that he had killed a man for simply snoring to loud. Matt was not related to John Wesley, but because he was called on to act as a lawman occasionally, it was to his advantage to let people think he was. After all, who would antagonize a man whose brother, who was never far away, had killed 10 or more men before his 20th birthday? Because of his past experience as a lawman, Matt was called on to settle more than one dispute.

On one occasion, a neighbor's twelve-year-old son had come to his home crying and telling Matt he needed help. The boy's name was Paul Landry, the son of Charles and Anna Landry, who lived just a short distance down river. Paul told him his pa was beating his mother and would he please come right away. Matt knew the boy and of his father's reputation as a drinker and a bully, so he left immediately to check on the woman.

When he arrived, the boy's father had already passed out and his wife Anna answered the door. It was obvious she had been beaten badly. Her left eye was bruised and turning dark and her lip was still bleeding. She told Matt her husband had quite a bit to drink. They had gotten into an argument about some work he had promised to do on the house and he slapped her. When she complained about his abuse in front of their son he told her the boy could use the education and hit her with his fist, knocking her to the floor. He told his son that a little discipline would always keep a woman in line. He then went to the bedroom and slammed the door shut behind him.

Matt asked Anna Landry if he did this often and she said he had started hitting her about a year earlier, but he was getting much worse as he had recently started drinking more. Matt suggested that she try to keep him off the whiskey and that he would talk to her husband Charles the following day when he sobered up.

The next morning Matt returned and had a long talk with Charles. Matt told him he was not acting in a legal capacity but he warned him about abusing his wife. He told him that he didn't take too kindly to a man beating a woman for any reason and if it happened again Charles would have to answer to him.

Things were quiet for a few weeks and then Paul came to him again. The boy was hysterical and told Matt that his pa had gotten real mean again. He had killed the boy's dog and two of its four pups. He had severely beaten and kicked the boy's mother and threatened to kill her too. His father had finished his whiskey and passed out.

Matt returned with the boy and found Anna badly injured. Her face was bloody and she may have suffered some broken ribs from being kicked. Anna told Matt that Charles had been pretty nice to her since his last visit. She had managed to keep him off the whiskey for the most part but they had another argument and he used that as an excuse to start drinking heavily. She had tried to reason with him but he had only gotten worse. When he started beating her, their dog had gotten between them trying to protect her from further injuries. He went for her again and the dog growled and stood his ground. He tripped and fell over the dog and in a rage had taken a fire poker and killed it. He then went after the dog's four pups saying he didn't want any damn dogs in the house anyway. Paul had managed to grab two of the pups and run outside with them. After killing the other two pups Charles went after his wife again. She was still on the floor. He kicked her one last time, warned her to keep her mouth shut about the incident and retreated to the bedroom.

After arriving at the Landry's place, Matt sent the boy to get Liz to look after Anna and then put on a pot of coffee. With Anna's permission, he took the three dead dogs out behind the house and buried them. By now the coffee was done and Anna had cleaned up some of the blood from the floor. Matt went to the bedroom and dragged Charles out of the bedroom and made him sit at the table and drink coffee. Charles wasn't too happy but he was afraid to put up to much of a fuss.

Liz had arrived with Paul, and was looking after Anna. She had cleaned up her face as best she could and wrapped her ribs with a torn bed sheet. They would try to get a doctor to see her later.

Charles finished the pot of coffee and when Matt figured he was sober enough, he took him outside to a small tool shed. They went inside and Matt immediately slapped him hard across the face. Charles groaned but did nothing else. Matt asked him how it felt. "Hell, what do you think?" Charles answered. Matt slapped him again.

Charles cursed. "Damn you. You know I can't fight you. You're the same as the law around here." "You don't see any badges do you?" said Matt and slapped him again. That was more than Charles could endure and he finally decided to fight back. He rook a futile swing at Matt. The boy, who had been looking from the door of the house, thought he had just witnessed an explosion. The whole side of the shed seemed to blow out followed by his father's body. Matt stepped through the hole in the shed and picked up Charles. When Charles was able to stand without Matt's support, he was promptly knocked down again. When Charles could no longer stand on his own, Matt figured he had enough. He picked him up and carried him into the house. There he laid him across the bed. "Now Charles," he said, "I think you know that I don't want to be called back here again."

Matt then turned to Anna and said, "Charles should be fine in a couple of days. "I will come back tomorrow to look in on you and the boy and repair your shed. Liz will stay here for a while and I will try to locate a doctor."

"Wait a minute," said Anna. "Thank you Mr. Hardin. I know it's not much but it's all we have." She gave Matt one of the pups and followed him to the door. Neither Anna or Paul had to call for Matt's help again and Charles Landry was a model citizen from that day forward. Matt would never wear a badge, but he was still the closest thing to a lawman that they had in the small town of Sometimes.

CHAPTER 6
Sometimes

Mary had just finished doing the breakfast dishes. Her daughter Elizabeth was going out the door and as the door slammed she yelled back over her shoulders, "I'm going fishing for a while." Mary smiled to herself as she thought about her pretty Liz, ten years old and a tom boy through and through. If she wasn't helping with chores she was fishing or hunting or doing anything else that would take her to the woods. She had always been a good child, seldom underfoot, but always a joy when she was. She had brought so much happiness into her life. She was her first child and because of complications during childbirth, her last. It was difficult to imagine a life without her lovely Liz.

She swept the kitchen floor and then grabbed the water bucket and left for the well. Her husband Mathew was busy cutting wood not too far from the well. Mathew or Matt as she called him was a big man and made most jobs look easy. He had already cut a big stack of wood and paused to watch Mary as she passed. How he loved that woman, so beautiful and forever young. "Do you need help with that bucket?" he asked, already knowing the answer. "I think I can handle it." Mary replied and gave a little skip to show off as well.

"Where was Liz going?" Matt asked. "She said she was going fishing." answered Mary. That got Matt's attention. "You better go get her, that darn rivers on the rampage. They must have had a hell of a rain up river." he said. "It won't be safe for her down there alone." Mary knew he was right. She put the bucket down and headed for the river.

She hadn't gone fifty yards when she heard the first scream. Liz was obviously in serious trouble. She turned long enough to make sure Matt had heard the yell for help also and then went for the river at a full run.

She heard another desperate yell for help just as she reached the swollen river. She could see where the river bank had crumbled and *Liz* had slipped several feet in the water. She looked down stream and saw a small hand reaching skyward from the surface of the river. Now the hand was gone and there was only water. Mary ran frantically now and dove into the river just past where her daughters hand had disappeared.

By now Matt had arrived and ran to the river's edge where Mary had gone in. She was under the water for an eternity, but finally broke the surface further down the river. She had Liz and was trying desperately to push her towards the river's edge. Matt ran towards Mary as she struggled to get to shore. Each *time* Mary pushed Liz towards shore the river carried them further downstream.

Mary was completely exhausted and with all her remaining strength pushed Liz into Matt's outstretched arms. Matt pulled Liz to safety and then looked to see that Mary was now under water. He dove into the water and searched for Mary but she was gone. As he searched, he screamed "Mary, Mary, Mary!" But there would be no answer. Then he was awake and Liz was saying "wake up pa, you're having another bad dream."

Even though it had been years since the tragic accident, the dreams still haunted him. It was 1875. Liz was twenty years old now and though she was a beautiful woman, she still acted like a child in many ways. She had swallowed a great deal of water on that terrible day before her mother found her and was finally able to shove her into his waiting arms. The doctors, and there had been many, said she had suffered *some b*rain damage from lack of oxygen. It *became* more apparent as she grew older. She was not as bright as others her age and it took her much longer to learn new skills. She had experienced *some* memory loss, but in many ways that was a blessing, for she never remembered the accident. She had been unconscious for several hours after being pulled from the water. Later, Matt had a very difficult time explaining what had happened to her mother, especially since her body was never recovered. Naturally, Liz had taken it very hard and blamed herself for her mother's death. It took many years for her to forgive herself and, of course, this had added further to her problems. She kept to herself and had no real close friends. The first few months especially were filled with dark depression. Matt had to keep a close *eye* on her for a very long time. She was doing much better now and had *become* a real asset to the household. She was a wonderful cook and kept the place spotless.

Matt had not remarried, partly out of grief, but mostly because there just were not too many women available in the small town of Sometimes. There were less than 100 people in the whole town and that was counting company. It was really just a farming community with most of the homes spread out along the river and just a few making up the town itself. There was only one place in town to get provisions and that was the general store. It also acted as a livery and if you played your cards right you could get coffee and a simple meal.

If you were able to get any food it was usually prepared by Liz. She also helped in the general store by stocking shelves and keeping the place presentable. She was never able to understand mathematics so she didn't handle the money or register at all. Matt's place was only about a quarter of a mile from town, so it was just a short walk and therefore convenient for her when she was needed.

Jack Taylor and his wife Carmine owned the general store and ran it with the help of their two sons. William was 14 and his older brother Jack Jr. was almost 18. When they needed extra help, they simply sent one of their boys on the trot to get Liz.

For Carmine, Liz was like the daughter she had always wanted but never had. On rare occasions, the stage might stop long enough for them require her help, but normally the stage was there for no more than a few minutes.

When the stage came from the south and got close to town, the driver would ask the passengers if they could hold their water for 30 minutes, for that was how long it would take to get to San Antonio. If they said yes, the stage would not stop, unless it was flagged down by Jack Taylor or someone looking for a ride into San Antonio. If they said no, they would stop at the general store and the suffering passengers would be allowed to visit the stores outhouse while other passengers took advantage of the break to stretch and visit the store. That was how the small town got its name. Sometimes the stage stopped there and at other times it just passed them by.

The stages came from as far south as Corpus Christi or even Mexico. From San Antonio you could proceed north to Austin or go west to El Paso or East to Houston and Galveston. In any event it was usually a long, hot, dusty and uncomfortable ride. Many men preferred a good horse over a stage because they had more say about their stops and certainly more say about their company along the way. The inside of a coach could get very close and more than one passenger had opted to ride on top with the luggage, or next to the driver if there was enough room. Even the finest gentleman often drank and smoked some pretty foul cigars on board. Enough on transportation of the day, and back to our story.

Even though San Antonio was only a 30 minutes ride from Sometimes, Matt had only been there a few times. Usually it was an opportunity for him to make a little money working for Jack Taylor. He took a wagon into San Antonio to pick up supplies for the store. Small quantities often came by stage and that was another time the stage stopped when traveling south. Real large shipments of goods were often delivered by the seller.

Matt usually traveled to San Antonio alone, but Liz accompanied him once just to see the big city. It had been an exciting time for her and the only time she would ever leave the farm.

Matt and Liz managed the farm alone. They had a few head of cattle, some horses and the usual small farm animals; chickens, turkeys and some guinea fowl. Of course, there were plenty of wild birds such as ducks, quail and turkey along the river. The deer were plentiful as well and a good substitute for beef on occasion.

Because he and Liz helped out at the general store he could count on the Taylor's help when he needed it. There were other neighbors as well and like most small communities they were all reasonably close and could be counted on in any emergency.

Matt would never get rich on his small place but he and Liz would get by okay. Matt was too busy working the farm or working with the Taylors to become bored and Liz had always been thrilled to live in the country. Sometimes was a quiet and peaceful little town and Matt and Liz were both very happy there.

CHAPTER 7
Old Mexico

In a small town just south of the Rio Grande, two men sat at a table at the rear of a small saloon. Other than the bartender, they were the only ones in the place. Most local customers had long since quit going into the bar. Only a few dared to enter and they never went alone. This was usually a very quiet town and people in the area, mostly Mexicans, didn't want anything to do with the two men who had been in town less than a week and who had been nothing but trouble since their arrival.

They had paid off the local lawman, a man by the name of Valdez, to make sure they wouldn't be bothered by him or anyone else while in town. They had made the saloon, not only a source of entertainment for them, but their hotel as well. They took over a couple of rooms in the rear of the building and spent most of the day drinking, eating and gambling right there in the saloon. They had no need to go anywhere else. Whatever they wanted they ordered from the bartender. By now they simply had to snap their fingers and the bartender jumped.

At first, they had no trouble getting local women to visit the place and take care of their personal needs, but even that was not possible now. They had abused the women so much they refused to return for any amount of money. One had been cut and beaten unconscious before she was carried to safety by the bartender. Her family's complaints fell on deaf ears and their unwelcome stay continued.

They were drinking now, and although it was early in the day, were well on their way to being drunk. They were both lean men of medium build. One was half-white and half-Indian and could have passed for a Mexican, except he spoke no Spanish. He may have been a half breed but few men dared to say it to his face. He went by the name of Wolf. He refused to take a regular job and didn't mind stealing or even killing to get whatever he wanted to stay alive. By the time he was twenty he had quite a reputation and was wanted by the law in Texas, Louisiana, and the territory of New Mexico.

The second man at the table was Mexican and at times like these did most of the talking for both of them. His name was Armando Reyes and he went by the name of Reyes. Like Wolf, he had been born in the territory of New Mexico. After killing his father, he had fled to Mexico. There he soon became proficient with most firearms but favored the knife because it was quiet and very personal. He was unstable enough to really appreciate the personal quality.

He didn't dare return to New Mexico, so after a few years he entered Texas by way of Juarez. He had a disagreement with a cowboy over the ownership of a horse. The cowboy called him a thieving greaser and started to take custody of the horse. He turned his back on Reyes and that was a fatal mistake. He fell to the ground with his throat cut and Reyes took the horse in question and promptly returned to Mexico.

He made his way to Laredo on the Texas side of the border. He got in trouble in Laredo fighting over the attentions of a pretty young lady in a bar. He was disarmed before he could do any serious harm to anyone and arrested.

It was in the Laredo jail where he met Wolf Smolly. They shared a cell, and because of their similar backgrounds soon became friends. The authorities did not yet know either man was wanted for murder in Texas or they would have put them in chains.

Shortly after Reyes's arrest, a third man was placed in their cell. A bunch of cowboys from out of town were celebrating and got a little too rowdy. When asked to settle down they all complied except the one who threatened one of the lawmen. He was disarmed, arrested and later beaten by deputies. Because the jail was so crowded, he was thrown in the same cell with the Mexican and the half-breed.

The cowboy, now sober, promised to be "out of that jail by morning." Later that evening his friends broke him out. They forced their way into the jail, overpowered the only deputy on duty, knocked him unconscious and took his keys. They unlocked the cell door and left town with their friend in quite a hurry. Reyes and Wolf, finding themselves unsupervised, promptly left the jail and crossed the Rio Grande to temporary safety.

Now, in the small Mexican town about 50 miles from Laredo they enjoyed relative freedom and felt unthreatened by the law. The peace would not last however, and they were soon visited by Valdez.

He entered the saloon, along with another Mexican carrying a shotgun, and told Reyes it would be necessary for them to leave town. The girl they had beaten and cut had died from her injuries. Several members of the girl's family had visited him at his of6ce and complained. They also threatened to lynch him along with the two murderers if he didn't arrest them. If they left now, he would tell the family that the two men had left before he could arrest them. Reyes explained to Wolf what he had been told and Wolf cursed. They both complained about all the money they had given to Valdez. They were informed that most of the money was gone and any that was left would be given to the girl's family. They continued to curse and threaten Valdez but they knew they had worn out their welcome.

Another Mexican entered the bar and told Valdez a mob was forming at the other end of town. That was all Reyes needed to hear. He told Wolf he was leaving immediately with or without him. It didn't take Wolf long to make up his mind. They both grabbed what few things they had, took two horses and never looked back.

They returned to Laredo but stayed on the Mexican side while they tried to decide their next move. By this time Reyes called his partner Lobo and since Wolf could not pronounce Reyes correctly, so they settled on Rey. The two managed to stay out of serious trouble for a while, but their past quickly caught up with them. The word was out that two men had killed a girl not far from here and the authorities had started asking questions.

It was time to move on, but where? They really had few choices. Wolf had suggested Arkansas, but Reyes said no. He had heard too much about Judge Parker in Arkansas. In fact, Judge Isaac Parker was a federal district judge working out of Fort Smith. He had a reputation as a hanging judge and apparently it was well deserved. During his tenure he sentenced more than 170 people to be hanged, including

4 women. Neither Wolf or Reyes wished to enhance his reputation.

They finally settled on the Oklahoma territory. There were plenty of places in Oklahoma where a man could get lost and there was little law in most of the territory. It meant a long trip through Texas where they were already wanted, but they had no time for long debates on the subject. Mexico was getting very hot in more ways than one. Besides, Texas was a large state with plenty of room for them to travel unnoticed by the law. Now out of money, the two men gathered some supplies, stole two of the best horses they could find and headed north across the Rio Grande and into South Texas open range.

CHAPTER 8
South Texas Ranch

The two men traveled along the road from Laredo to San Antonio, avoiding any populated areas as they went. Whenever they saw a wagon, stage or any other riders approaching, they left the road until the other travelers were gone. This slowed them down somewhat, but they did not want to draw any attention to themselves for obvious reasons.

The first day was uneventful and they made camp for the night, a good distance off the road. They made no fire and rose early the next morning to resume their journey. They rode all day until late afternoon. They had just passed a large ranch when Reyes's horse went lame.

Now, they were in a fix. With one horse they would either have to ride double or one of them would have to walk. This was going to be much too slow and neither man wanted to walk. But, no matter, Wolf had a plan. They would return to the ranch they had just passed and steal a horse and whatever else they needed. That sounded good to Reyes so they backtracked to the road that led to the ranch house.

As they neared the house, they knew their timing had been bad. It was nearing dark and the ranch owner along with most of his hands had already returned from their chores for the day. The entire outfit had been gathering and branding cattle for several days. Reyes and Wolf passed a large bunkhouse, but before they got within 50 yards of the house they were challenged by an old Mexican. He asked them who they were and what they wanted. Reyes answered him in Spanish, telling him their names were Reyes and Smolly. He told the man they had lost a horse and had much too far to go to proceed on foot.

The old man identified himself as Victorio Sanchez the caretaker of the place. Victoria took great pride in the fact that when the ranch owner was gone, he looked after the house and the rest of the owner's family. Victoria's wife kept the ranch house clean and did most of the cooking. Victoria and his wife lived in a small house behind the main house.

Victoria told Reyes that the owner, Mr. Jacobs, was having his evening meal and could talk to them after finishing his meal. Bur Walter Jacobs was already on the porch and came out to see what was going on. As he approached the trio, he asked the old man for an explanation. Victorio responded by saying the two men had lost one of their horses and needed help.

"We don't normally sell horses, for as you can see, we are in the cattle business." said the rancher. "I need all my good horses here on the ranch. If you really need one, I could probably sell you a pack horse." he said. Reyes told him they had come on hard times and had no money, almost no food and little of value. The rancher nodded to Victorio and the two men walked off a short distance to discuss the situation.

Before Walter could speak, the old man told him he didn't trust the two and were sure they were up to no good. The rancher echoed his remarks and told Victorio that he would not give them a horse. They were welcome to stay the night and if they were hungry, they could get some food at the bunkhouse. If they decided to spend the night on the ranch, he wanted them watched constantly. Furthermore, they would be escorted to the main road early the next day. The rancher returned to the house to finish his meal and Victorio was left to explain their decision to Reyes.

Reyes was furious. No one had ever treated him like this and not regretted it. But what could they do, they were badly outnumbered, had no money to buy a horse and it was obvious there would be no charity here. They told Victorio they would like to spend the night and have a meal, so he took them to bunkhouse and introduced them to the ranch foreman. Victorio asked the foreman to see that the two men had a meal and a place to stay for the night.

Later, while the two were eating, Victorio explained to the foreman that Mr. Jacobs wanted the two men watched all night and escorted to the ranch entrance in the morning. The foreman assured him it would be done and that he would talk to Walter in the morning.

Wolf and Reyes finished their meal and the foreman showed them a place in the barn where they would be comfortable for the night. There was no room in the bunkhouse but it mattered little. The foreman didn't want them bunking with the rest of the men anyway. Where he put them, they could easily be watched until morning. A ranch hand woke them early the next day and took them to the bunkhouse for breakfast. After breakfast they gathered their things along with their one horse and were shown the gate. Their escort watched them travel north until they were out of sight. He then returned and reported to the foreman who was talking to Jacobs and planning their day.

They had decided that Jacobs, the foreman, and the other hands would resume their normal chores but they would leave one hand to stay near the house with Victoria. Jacobs felt it necessary for security reasons. He thought the two transients might return and try to steal a horse. The foreman turned to the young cowboy and told him to remain near the bunkhouse and keep an eye on the horses. He could help the cook around the bunkhouse and clean up the tack room if he had time. Jacobs returned to the house, talked to Victorio for a while and then left with the foreman and the rest of the ranch hands to continue their branding.

Their departure did not go unobserved. Reyes and Wolf had turned back to the ranch as soon as they knew they were out of sight. They would simply watch the place for a while and then they would have their way. They knew the old Mexican would be there along with the rancher's family. They later saw the cook and another man. The other man was the same young cowboy that had escorted them to the gate. They watched for a while longer and after seeing no others, approached the rear of the bunkhouse on foot.

Now Reyes's skill with the knife would prove invaluable to the killers. Reyes cautioned Wolf to use a gun only if he had to. They waited for the young cowboy to leave the bunkhouse. Reyes followed him into the barn. When Reyes left the barn, the young man was dead, laying in a pool of blood with his throat cut. Reyes then stealthily entered the bunkhouse where the cook suffered the same fate. The two killers could now take horses and supplies and leave without resistance but Reyes would have none of it. "Come on Rey, lets go. We have everything we need right here." said Wolf. Rey replied, "My work here isn't finished and my play neither." "I won't leave until I cut that smart Mexican down to size." "You can stay here Lobo, but I am going to the house."

Wolf followed Reyes to the rear of the ranch house. They found the old Mexican and his wife in their small home where they surprised them. They were inside before the old couple could get up from the table where Victoria was drinking coffee. "Remember me pancho?" said Reyes grinning. Victoria tried to go for a rifle hanging near the door, but Reyes pounced on him like a cat, yelling, "Tell me again why I can't have a horse." With that he ended the old man's life. Victoria's wife started to scream but she also was silenced instantly by Reyes. The two men looked around the little house but could find nothing worth taking, so they turned their attentions to the ranch house.

They found the rancher's wife in a sewing room with her son who looked to be about 10 years old. They brutally raped and murdered the woman while the young boy watched. They then ransacked the house. They found a cash box in a desk. Inside was some paper money and a considerable number of 20 dollar gold pieces. They took the money and a few other things they wanted and returned to the bunkhouse. At the bunkhouse they helped themselves to food and supplies and other goods.

They returned to the main road and turned south. They made sure the tracks were clear as they knew they would be followed. They wanted anyone following them to think they were headed for Mexico. After about a mile, they left the main road and turned back north. They would stay well off the road now until they were clear of the ranch they had plundered.

Walter Jacobs and his men returned from their work that evening to find a bloody scene, first at the barn and bunkhouse and finally at the main house. They found the young boy near the lifeless body of his mother. They questioned the boy but he was no help, as he had gone into shock. But it wasn't difficult to figure out who was responsible for the carnage. Walter sent two of his hands to try to track the killers. He also sent one of his best riders to Laredo to report the killings to the Marshall.

Then, the rest of the men began cleaning the place up and preparing the bodies for burial. The two, trackers, returned after a couple of hours and told Walter that the two killers had turned south and were probably well on their way to Mexico by now. If the murderers stayed on the main road the rider headed for Laredo might even see them.

The Marshall from Laredo arrived at the ranch the following day. He compared notes with Walter, and based on descriptions given by the rancher and the foreman, concluded that the two men responsible for these murders were the same two that had escaped from jail a few weeks earlier. By now the Marshall knew the killers were both wanted in Texas and Mexico as well. If they returned to Mexico it would not be by way of Laredo, he was sure of that.

Walter told the Marshall, "I want these blood thirsty bastards dead. I want you to post a reward of 500 dollars on each man. I will make payment when they are arrested and prosecuted or on proof of their death. If they are prosecuted, I want to be there when they hang." The Marshall assured him he would handle the matter personally and would make every effort to make sure the killers were brought to justice quickly.

But Reyes and Wolf were survivors and would be difficult to catch. There would be no quick justice.

CHAPTER 9
Moving North

Reyes and Wolf traveled much slower now. They didn't dare travel too close to the road for fear of being seen. There was no doubt in their mind that a lot of people were looking for them, not only the law, but others as well. They had good horses and plenty of supplies but traveling the brush country of South Texas was difficult at best. They were lucky to make 20 miles a day and that was riding from daylight to dark. They had to rest the horses occasionally because of the heat and their need for water but Wolf rode like he had a map in his head and could instinctively find water.

Wolf became nervous and edgy and told Reyes he was sure they were being followed. They tried to move a little faster but Wolf was still uneasy. "We can make a run for it or make a stand right here." said Wolf Neither option was very appealing. They couldn't move much faster and there was no good place to take cover for a fight. Reyes said, "Relax Lobo. Have a drink and let's keep moving. You're going loco on me."

After a short distance Wolf told Reyes to look to his right and then to his left. There were riders on both sides. "Now Rey, am I seeing things too?" said Wolf. The riders slowly closed in on both sides and now the two men could see they were Indians. There were at least a dozen of them and running now was not an option. They dismounted and took cover behind their horses. There was nothing to do but wait for the Indians to make the first move. As they got closer Wolf could see that this band of Indians wasn't looking for a fight. It was a rag tag band of renegade Apache and they looked like death warmed over. When they got close enough, Wolf yelled to them in his Comanche tongue but got no response. He told Reyes to hold his fire and stepped out from behind the horses and greeted them in sign language. One of the Indians responded with a friendly greeting. Wolf asked him what they wanted. The Indian told him they were being hunted by the army and if they were caught, they would be jailed or forced to live on a reservation. They were hungry and there would be no need for a fight if they could have their pack horses. Wolf and Reyes both knew they had no choice in the matter. They were outnumbered and if they decided to fight there would be a lot of bloodshed and some of it would be theirs. The Indians left with the pack horses and Reyes and Wolf proceeded north. They could always steal more horses, but hair was hard to come by.

After a couple of days of riding, they crossed another large ranch. They never saw a ranch house, but they found good water with some cattle nearby. They killed a young steer and risked a fire during the day to have a feast.

The fresh beef was a very pleasant change in diet, so they spent most of the day just resting and eating. In the late afternoon Wolf spotted a lone rider in the distance. He wasn't sure if the man had seen them or not but they would take no chances. They packed their things and moved north several miles before making camp for the night. This extra precaution may have saved them from an early lynching.

Ranchers didn't take kindly to having their cattle butchered by people passing through their property, fenced or not, especially since there was plenty of deer and other wild game available.

The lone rider had seen them and had returned to the ranch's main house to inform the owner of the sighting. The word about the ranch killings had spread like wildfire and no one was taking any chances. Several ranch hands had returned that same evening to the place where the two killers had been sighted. They found the cook fire and what was left of the steer but it was growing dark so the men returned to the ranch house. They couldn't be sure who the two men were that had killed the steer. It could have been almost anyone. It was not unusual for wetbacks or illegal immigrants to cross the property in their travels but they seldom killed any cattle. In any case, the sighting was not considered important enough to bother the authorities.

The following morning two ranch hands returned to the place where the steer had been killed. One of the men was a fair tracker. They followed the transients' trail and found where they had spent the night. They tracked them for several more hours until they reached the ranch's north boundary. At this time, they left the track and returned to the ranch house as instructed. They had satisfied themselves that they would not be bothered further by the two men who seemed to be continuing north.

Travel for the two was easier now. There was more grass and less brush and of course more water as they moved north towards San Antonio. They had been traveling to the west of the main road so as they neared San Antonio they swung west to bypass the city. After San Antonio they rode northeast in the direction of Austin. They continued to travel off the main road for several days. They never had a fire at night and that meant a lot of cold meals.

One morning Wolf killed a deer. They built a fire to cook the venison and remained at that site the rest of the day relaxing and eating. They were in no hurry now, as there was plenty of water and game and they were confident there was no one following them. The horses were doing well. They still had plenty of supplies and life was good for the two men. After a few more days they had bypassed Austin. The hill country was beautiful with plenty of rivers and creeks to camp near, but Reyes was getting bored. He craved some excitement. He was tired of eating venison or cold meals from a can. What he really wanted was some whiskey and women. Wolf assured him there was plenty of both waiting for them in Oklahoma, but Oklahoma was weeks away and that seemed like a lifetime to Reyes.

One day out of Austin they saw a group of riders in the distant so they took cover and watched as a column of cavalry passed within 200 yards of them. Wolf thought they may have been from Fort McKavett or Fort Concho, but if so, they were a long way from home. Sights like this were rare now. Most forts were now abandoned because Indians were less of a threat. Most of them had been rounded up and placed on reservations, but soldiers were still needed occasionally to keep the peace, partly because of renegades like Reyes and Wolf. After the column was well out of sight they proceeded on their journey.

In a few more days they would be near Waco. They would have to stop there, if not before, for more supplies. Nothing could make Reyes happier. He complained constantly about being bored, hungry or thirsty, and it wasn't water he wanted. They had been on the move now for weeks and both men were saddle weary. When they saw a small town on the Bosque River just west of Waco, they agreed they would stop and get supplies. Wolf told Reyes to remain outside of town while he went for supplies. He didn't think it would be too smart for the two men to be seen together. Reyes did not take too kindly to that idea and said he wanted to go into town for a few drinks. Wolf knew this meant trouble for sure and told Reyes he would buy plenty of whiskey and bring it to him. After a great deal of arguing Reyes finally agreed to remain behind.

Wolf left Reyes in a small grove of oak trees and with the pack horse proceeded into town. There was one saloon, two general stores and very little else. He entered the small saloon and ordered a whiskey. The place was almost deserted. A few men playing cards, one other man at the bar and of course a couple of girls to work the customers. One of the girls approached him and asked if he would buy her a drink. He wasn't interested and told her so. After he finished his drink, he purchased two bottles of whiskey to take with him. He then went to the nearest general store and got enough provisions to last a couple of weeks. He took a different route out of town and then doubled back for Reyes.

When he arrived at the oak grove Reyes was gone. It wasn't too hard to figure out where he might have gone. He decided to give Reyes a little time in town and waited for his return. After several hours it became obvious he would have to go find Reyes so he returned to the saloon. He didn't see his horse but entered and inquired at the bar about his friend. The bartender knew immediately who he was looking for. The bartender said the Mexican had come in earlier and ordered whiskey. He had also purchased several drinks for one of the girls. After a great deal of drinking the Mexican had offered to take the girl to the back for some private entertainment. The girl didn't like his looks and told him so. This really angered the Mexican, who said something like, "You whore, you drank my whiskey and now you don't want my company." He then hit her in the face with his fist. The girl went down hard. She screamed some obscenities and started to get up. The Mexican would have hit her again but the bartender hit him with a billy club, and that was the end of the fray. The bartender told Wolf the Mexican would be easy to find as he had been arrested and locked up after he came to. The jail was just down the street. Wolf cursed to himself as he left the bar. This was the attention they didn't need. Reyes was starting to get on his nerves. He knew Reyes would be drunk and decided to let him sleep it off.

He made camp in the oak grove for the night. The following morning he went to the town jail. There was a deputy sitting behind an old wooden desk drinking a cup of coffee. He asked Wolf what he needed. Wolf replied, 'I'm looking for a friend of mine, I was told he might be here in jail." The deputy answered, "I didn't think this Mexican we got locked up had any friends. He is one loco son of a bitch. What do you want with him?" Wolf said, "I was hoping to get him out of jail." The deputy said, "He ain't going nowhere. He beat up a lady and broke her jaw. On top of a big fine, he has to pay doctor bills too." Wolf asked, "How much will all that come to?" "I can't help you there. You will have to talk to the sheriff." answered the deputy.

"He's across the street having breakfast." About that time Reyes yelled from a cell in another room, "When do I get breakfast?" "When I get damn good and ready to get it for you, and right now I ain't ready." yelled the deputy.

Wolf left and walked across the street to the cafe. The sheriff had just finished his meal and was drinking coffee. Wolf approached the table and asked if he could sit. The sheriff nodded and pointed to a chair. Wolf sat and explained his situation. The sheriff told him there would be a fine and doctor's expenses. Wolf asked, "Do you think $20 would cover it?" "I don't know." said the sheriff. "The doctor had to wire up the girls jaw and she lost a tooth. The judge would have to decide the amount of the fine. But I think $40 would just about cover everything and we wouldn't have to wait for a judge. I could let your friend out right away." said the sheriff. Wolf knew if he wanted Reyes out of jail right away, he better give the sheriff what he wanted, so he agreed. "Let's go to my office and settle up." said the sheriff.

They walked back to the jail where the sheriff told the deputy to go get some breakfast. After the deputy left, the sheriff took the money. He then asked Wolf where the two men were from and where they were headed. Wolf told him they were from San Antonio and were headed for Oklahoma to visit friends and find work. The sheriff went to the back room, unlocked the cell and brought out Reyes. He explained to both of them they were no longer welcome in town and he expected them to leave immediately. Reyes grinned at the sheriff and said, "I guess this means I ain't getting no breakfast." "You guessed right, and I wouldn't wait around for dinner either." said the sheriff. Reyes took his belongings and the two men left for the livery to get

Reyes's horse. They wasted no time getting out of town and headed north again for Oklahoma.

Reyes immediately started complaining about not having anything to eat. Wolf said, "Damn you Rey, shut up! You can have the same thing I had for breakfast, cold beans with a whiskey chaser, and while you're at it why not hang a sign on your back (wanted dead or alive for murder) you stupid fool." The two men rode in silence. Wolf was really angry and Reyes knew it.

CHAPTER 10
The Possee

The deputy, now very excited, returned from breakfast and asked the sheriff about the prisoner. The sheriff told him that his friend had paid a fine to get him out of jail and they had left for Oklahoma. The deputy chuckled and said, "I hope you got plenty of money because those two men are probably worth $1000.00. I was just talking to a fellow from Waco. After hearing about the Mexican and his partner he said they sounded like the two men wanted in South Texas for murder. The fellow saw a poster in Waco on the two men, a Mexican and a breed. They killed several people on a ranch, but the law thought that they went to Mexico."

The sheriff said, "I guess we screwed up pretty bad, huh." The deputy responded, "If you give me half the money you took off that fella, you can say we screwed up, otherwise, you screwed up." "Don't worry about that now," said the sheriff "Round up a few men for a posse and we'll go after them and send a man to Waco and let the Marshal there know about the two men. He may want to send out some men too. And please don't tell him we had one of them locked up."

As soon as they were ready, the sheriff, his deputy and three other men, now also deputized, headed north in hopes of catching up with Reyes and Wolf. They wanted the reward money and didn't care how they got it. The poster said dead or alive and dead men don't talk. The sheriff knew he had made a big mistake and didn't want everyone in Texas to know about it.

By the end of the day, there were at least three groups of men looking for the two killers. The Marshal in Waco had formed a posse. A vigilante group, more interested in the reward than justice, had also left Waco and joined the hunt.

Reyes and Wolf would not be easy to catch. They were as cunning as a couple of coyotes and had plenty of supplies. They were watching their backs and knew if they crossed the Red River into Oklahoma territory the law would probably turn back. They rode steadily for a few hours and that was when Wolf realized they had company. The posse, with the sheriff, deputy and three other men, were approaching from the south at a gallop. They spurred their horses and the chase was on. They stayed well ahead of the posse all day. Once it was dark, the posse had to give up the chase until the morning. Reyes and Wolf rode for several more hours before stopping.

The horses needed a rest as bad as they did. At daylight they proceeded at a slower pace since they had a good lead on the posse. By that afternoon the posse was sighted and again they pushed their horses to stay ahead of their pursuers. They rode until after dark and were moving slowly when they saw a camp fire in the distance. Wolf assumed it was a second posse since it was easy to wire ahead and alert authorities in the area. They dismounted and quietly approached the campsite. Wolf got close enough to see four people sleeping around a small cook fire. He also counted four horses nearby. He assumed there was no sentry and he saw none.

They could have left and rode on, but knew they would have to deal with them sooner or later. Wolf gave Reyes the sign, a slashing motion across the throat, and turned him loose. Reyes was able to kill three of the four men without a sound. Suddenly, the fourth man jumped to his feet and was immediately shot by Wolf. It was over in less than three minutes. They helped themselves to a pot of beans still warm from the evening meal. They went through the pockets and saddle bags of the four men and took what they wanted. Two of the four horses looked especially good so they took them also and moved on.

They traveled for a couple of hours and then made camp, confident they were well ahead of the law. The following morning the posse that had been close behind them found the campsite with the four murdered men. The four were neither lawmen or vigilantes. They were simply four cowhands in the wrong place at the wrong time. The sheriff instructed one of his men to use the spare horses to carry the bodies to the nearest town and turn them over to authorities for possible identification and burial. There was little else to do for the deceased and the sheriff was even more determined to catch the killers now, no matter how hard it would be on the men and the horses.

The man assigned to carry the bodies was making his way south and was met by the Waco posse after only an hour. He explained to the marshal and the other six men with him what had happened. The men in the posse were unable to identify any of the men but the marshal was able to provide directions to Fort Worth. It was a half days ride from their present location but was better suited for the task ahead.

The Waco posse rode hard and eventually caught the other five men in pursuit of the killers. They agreed to join forces, as it was evident the two killers would not be easy to take under any circumstances. Depending on how hard the fugitives rode, they could reach the Red River and cross over into Oklahoma in a few days.

Wolf and Reyes played cat and mouse with their pursuers for two days. They were in no real hurry as they had the advantage. They could travel at night and put more distance between them because the posse could not track after dark. During the day they simply made sure the posse stayed out of sight most of the time. If they saw the posse getting too close they switched to fresh horses and rode hard until the posse was out of sight. They were hoping that once they crossed the Red River the posse would turn back.

On the morning of the third day, they were elated to see the Red River in the distance. They knew refuge was a short swim away. Their hopes were dashed, however, as they arrived at the river's edge. The Red River was on the rampage and well above flood stage. There would be no crossing the Red for some time and time was something they didn't have.

They decided to follow the river upstream for a while but even that proved hopeless. Wolf wanted to try to cross into Oklahoma territory by putting his horse in the lead and hanging on to the saddle but Reyes was terrified at the prospect. He couldn't swim and had no intentions of entering the water, horse or no horse. Even a lone horse could not have crossed the river that day, so the pair had little choice but to continue moving up river or turn south into the waiting hands of the posse. They chose to follow the Red upstream for a while in hopes of finding a crossing point. The more they rode, the more it became evident that Oklahoma would stay out of reach and the posse had the advantage now. They could follow the fugitives up river day and night. Time was running out for Reyes and Wolf and they both knew it.

CHAPTER 11
Returning South

Reyes and Wolf discussed their options, knowing the posse was now close on their heels. Oklahoma was now out of reach and they were wanted in every nearby state or territory except Arkansas. They wanted nothing to do with Judge Parker in Arkansas because of his reputation, so they elected to return to Mexico. At least there they would blend in with the populace and of course Reyes could speak the language. They had made it through Texas once and they could do it again. They proceeded up river for a few more miles and then turned south. They figured the posse would think they were headed for New Mexico or simply waiting for a chance to cross the river into Oklahoma.

After a day's ride south, they turned east to further throw off their pursuers. They hoped to put more distance between them and the posse bur nothing was working for the two men now. They spotted the posse on the second day and had to switch to fresh horses again to outdistance them. By now the number of men in the posse had dwindled to six. The others had grown tired of what seemed like a fruitless pursuit and returned home. Those who remained with the posse were more determined than ever and the fugitives were growing weary of this never-ending chase. The killers were also getting low on supplies and it would be necessary to stop and replenish their stock before too long. It was *time* to make a stand and end the chase one way or another.

They doubled back about a mile to a spot they had selected for an ambush. They put the horses out of sight in a nearby clump of trees and waited for the posse behind an outcropping of rock.

They didn't have to wait long. The posse approached with one man, obviously the tracker, slightly in the lead. Wolf had instructed Reyes to shoot the tracker and riders in the forefront. He would take care of the riders to the rear. The posse was caught in the open and from their vantage point Reyes and Wolf managed to bring down all of the riders but one. That rider was wounded, but made his escape, riding southwest at a gallop, with shots ringing out behind him. He would live to tell his story of the massacre but would never ride with another posse.

Reyes and Wolf took their time now and approached the downed riders cautiously. Two of the men were still alive. They shot them and went through the men's personal belongings taking any money and provisions they found. They could use the money to buy more supplies later. For now, they could relax, knowing that these men would be no further problem. The fact that they had just killed five men didn't bother them in the least. After all, they could only die once.

They gathered their horses and traveled south for several days. Along the way they were able to kill some deer and took time to enjoy some cooked meals. This was the first time they had dared to build a fire.

It would be a while before the posse's lone survivor got word back to Waco about the ambush. The authorities immediately put together another posse to avenge the loss of their comrades and bring the two killers to justice. By now posters on the two men were everywhere, and after the Waco posse was annihilated the reward for them was raised to $1000.00 per man. Rumors were flying now. There were reported sightings all over the state of Texas. Many people thought they were in Oklahoma and others swore the two men had been seen in New Mexico or Arkansas.

Vigilante groups and bounty hunters combed the countryside in hopes of collecting the reward, but Reyes and Wolf would be hard to find. By now they were experienced in eluding their would-be captors and had no intentions of being taken alive. The idea of strangling in a hangman's noose had no appeal to them at all. If they had to leave this world, it would be in a blaze of gunfire and they agreed to stay together now until they reached old Mexico. Once they did, they would part company. Wolf knew Reyes could not stay out of trouble long because his love for whiskey and women was too strong. He would have a better chance of survival without Reyes, no matter where he went after the two reached Mexico.

They proceeded south for two more days, constantly scanning the horizon for riders. Again, they stayed off the main road and were much more cautious, avoiding all populated areas and making sure they would not be seen by anyone. From now on there would be no more cook fires after dark. It was much too risky. As an added precaution, they kept two of the horses saddled and ready to go, in the event they were surprised at night. They still had two good spare horses and a good pack horse but it was time to replenish their food supplies and of course get some more whiskey.

They saw a small town and decided to get supplies there. Wolf told Reyes he would take the pack horse into town and get plenty of food and whiskey for the journey south. He also told Reyes to wait for him to return. If Reyes was not there when Wolf returned, he would leave without him. He would not bother looking for him this time. Reyes knew Wolf meant every word and didn't argue with him. When Wolf returned with the supplies the two proceeded south.

It wasn't long before they noticed a lone rider following them. Someone in the small town had apparently suspected Wolf of being one of the men the law was looking for and decided to check him out. It was probably one of the many bounty hunters now looking for the two killers. Unfortunately, it could also be the lead man or tracker for another posse. They kept an eye out for the rider and saw him several more times in the distance, but never saw a posse. As they suspected, it was a bounty hunter who had decided to go it alone and not share the reward with anyone, a fatal error on his part.

Reyes continued riding south with all the horses. Wolf remained behind out of sight of the approaching rider. The bounty hunter was wary and alert but once he was in rifle range, Wolf easily shot him off his horse. He then approached the rider cautiously to make sure he was dead. He went through the man's things and found a wanted poster for him and Reyes. He caught the man's horse and soon joined Reyes. He laughed about how easy it was to kill the bounty hunter and bragged that they were now both worth a thousand dollars.

They were well provisioned now and were able to move steadily south, avoiding contact with anyone. One of them was awake at all times, and because they never had a fire after dark, they were not in danger of being easily detected.

This was their life now for many days. At times one of them would catnap in the saddle but again one of them was always awake. They saw tracks and occasionally campsites of groups of men and suspected they were probably looking for them. They never saw any posse or vigilante groups but they knew they were out there scouring the area for them. Anyone foolish enough to get close enough to identify them was eliminated without question. The two killers had traveled a great distance now. They had left a trail of dead behind them, killing and stealing as they moved south to old Mexico. They had just skirted east around San Antonio and would have to stop soon. They were almost out of food and Reyes wanted more whiskey.

CHAPTER 12
Satan Visits Sometimes

It was mid morning, and Liz was doing general housekeeping chores when the two men entered the general store. Jack and Carmine were in the stockroom at the rear of the building. They were making room for a shipment of goods from San Antonio. Mathew and the Taylor's youngest son William had taken a wagon to pick up a special shipment of supplies and were expected back soon. The older son, Jack Jr., was helping out a farmer about two miles down river. The two boys often earned extra money by doing work for other families in their small town.

Liz was frightened by the two men's rough appearance, and even more so, by the way Reyes stared at her. She called for Carmine who came to the front of the store to see what Liz needed. Carmine knew immediately who the two men were. She had seen wanted posters on the two men when the posters had been circulated in the area. The two men saw the fear in Carmines eyes and knew she had recognized them. Wolf told Reyes, "No gun play." Carmine turned and yelled for Jack. She started to run for the stockroom but Reyes was on her before she could take a step. He ended her life with a slash across her throat. Jack came through the stockroom door, just in time to see Carmine collapse to the floor. He was stunned and for a moment frozen in disbelief. When he regained his composure he screamed in rage and attacked Reyes. Jack was stabbed, once in the stomach and was wrestling with Reyes for the knife when Wolf knocked him unconscious with his pistol.

Liz took advantage of the scuffle and made it out the door, running instinctively for home. As she neared the house, she called for her dog which now was her only help. The dog was quite large, being a mixture of collie and shepherd, and was very protective of Liz. They both made it through the door but never had a chance to secure it.

Reyes burst through the door knocking Liz to the floor. Wolf, being more cautious and not knowing who might be in the house, stayed a good distance back to see what would develop. The dog leaped upon Reyes as he came through the door, but he too fell under the knife. Reyes did a quick check of the house while Wolf waited outside.

Wolf yelled to Reyes, "Who's in there?" Reyes replied, "No one but my new bride." Wolf entered the house to find the dog whimpering on the floor and Reyes dragging Liz by her hair towards a bedroom. While Reyes had his way with *Liz,* Wolf looked around the house for anything of value.

Jack Taylor had regained consciousness and now staggered into the house with a rifle in his hands. He had heard Liz screaming and hoped he was not too late to help. In his dazed condition he would have been better off waiting for the two men to come out, but he could not ignore Liz's screams and pleas for mercy. Before he could use the rifle, he was clubbed again with Wolf's pistol, which opened a huge gash just above the left ear. He fell to the floor bleeding profusely.

Liz finally quit screaming and Reyes came out of the bedroom grinning. "It's your turn now," he told Wolf, laughing. When Wolf entered the room, he was not surprised to find Liz already dead, lying naked in an ever-widening pool of blood. Reyes had already gone outside to the well to wash up for he too was covered with blood. When Wolf came out of the bedroom the dog was still whimpering, and Jack, moaning from his wounds caught Wolf by the leg as he stepped over him. Wolf pulled free and drew his revolver. Jack begged him to finish the job. Wolf responded, "I don't like wasting powder, but I reckon I can afford one round." With that said, he pointed his pistol, first at Jack and then at the dog, and fired one shot. The dog stopped whimpering now, and Wolf went out the door laughing. There would be plenty of ammunition and supplies in the general store for the taking and Jack Taylor was in no condition to stop them.

The two men returned to the general store and helped themselves to enough provisions to take them to the Mexican border. They had grown bolder now and were confident they would soon reach the safety of old Mexico. To celebrate the occasion they broke open a bottle and had several drinks, toasting each other over the lifeless body of Carmine Taylor. The pair, with two extra horses and their pack horse loaded, crossed over the main road and headed south. Reyes, now well on his way to being drunk, turned and with a gleeful yell, gave a final salute with an empty bottle to the bloody scene behind them.

A few minutes later, Mathew and William returned from San Antonio with a wagon full of supplies. They pulled the wagon up next to the back entrance to the stock room. Mathew told William to take care of the horses and went into the stock room. From there he went on into the front of the store. What he found made him sick to his stomach. It was obvious he could do nothing for Carmine. He called out for Liz and Jack to no avail. He ran outside and headed for his house. As he ran past the wagon he yelled, "Will, stay out of the store and wait for me right there!"

He found Jack Sr. just inside the door. He looked dead. He yelled for Liz but got no answer. He went to the back room and found Liz and had to run outside. Now he was really ill. As he leaned against the house, he heard Jack Sr. calling for him. He went inside and kneeled down next to Jack. Jack could talk but he was very weak. He had lost a great deal of blood. Jack said he was cold so Matt got a blanket and pillow and tried to make him more comfortable.

Jack told him everything that had happened, at least how he knew it. He told about trying to save Liz and apologized for his failure. He told Matt how he asked the one man to finish him and what his response was. He said, "Mathew, those two men are devils. They are evil and don't deserve to live. Promise me you will hunt them down for me, for Carmine and for Liz. "It will be done." said Mathew. "Rest now and I will get you some help." "I didn't want to live earlier." said Jack. "Now I want to live for my sons and I know I can't." He continued. "Look after them for me,

Mathew." Mathew stepped outside trying to hold back the tears. He knew Jack would not live long.

He yelled out for William to go to the nearest neighbor and tell them they needed help right away and to go from there and get his brother and bring him back with him. Hopefully they would both return before their father died.

Mathew entered the back room again and covered Liz's body. He then closed the door and returned to the side of his dying friend. Jack again complained of being cold so Mathew added another blanket, knowing it would do no good. Before any help could arrive, his old friend would die in his arms.

When the first neighbor arrived, Mathew told him briefly what had happened. He told him to keep the two boys away from their parents, if he could, and away from Liz as well. It was difficult enough that the boys had lost their Mother and Father, Mathew did not want them to see the bloody carnage.

With that he left the house and started saddling his best horse. He took a spare horse and grabbed some supplies. He was ready to leave when Will and Jack Jr. returned. Before they could enter the house, he told Jack Jr. he was leaving things in his hands. The two boys would have the help of neighbors but he had to leave now.

Mathew had no time for details and there were no words to describe how he felt anyway. He mounted his horse and never looked back, as he rode off in pursuit of the two men who had just destroyed his world as he knew it.

CHAPTER 13
The Final Run

Mathew rode steady, hoping to catch the two killers before dark. The trail was easy to follow with their two extra horses and pack animal. He had ridden for about forty-five minutes, when he heard someone yelling his name. A lone rider came up behind him and Mathew could see it was Jack Jr. yelling frantically for him to hold. Jack Jr. told him he had seen the bloody work of the killers and had quickly saddled a horse. He said his goodbyes to his parents, knowing full well there was nothing he could do for them. He told Will and the others he had to at least try to get some justice for his family. Mathew would have preferred that the boy would have stayed at home with the others but he knew by the wild, angry, almost insane look on Jack Jrs. face that there was no turning him back now. He talked to the boy now as they rode on, trying to settle him down. He warned him of the danger ahead and of the need for caution. The men they were following were no better than animals and if cornered would be much more dangerous.

It was late afternoon and the two fugitives were moving slowly. First, because of their boldness, which now grew with every mile south and second, because Reyes could barely sit on his horse. Reyes had been drinking since they had left Sometimes. "Damn you Rey, you are so drunk you can barely ride. I am fed up with your drinking. Your drinking got you arrested before, and if it happens again I won't hang around to get you out. They will hang you for sure." said Wolf. Reyes was too drunk to listen to the lecture. When the two men finally came to a nice shaded area, Reyes insisted that they stop and rest for a while. Wolf reluctantly agreed, but only if Reyes would quit drinking. The two men dismounted and were resting under a large oak having a simple canned meal. Reyes was beginning to sober up when they saw the two riders approaching from the north.

They were no more surprised than Mathew. He had no idea he had gotten so close and now, here they were, right in front of him. He quickly dismounted and pulled his rifle from its scabbard. He fired wildly at the two men but was too excited to shoot accurately. Jack Jr. didn't slow down but instead brought his horse to a full gallop going straight for the two firing his pistol all the while. In a rage he still advanced even after he had emptied his pistol. Mathew could only look on in horror as Wolf took careful aim and shot the boy off his horse. Wolf and Reyes then mounted and rode south in a panic, leaving their pack horse and spare horses behind.

Mathew remounted and approached the place where Jack Jr. had fallen from his horse. Mathew dismounted and examined the body. He was shot in the breast and had died almost instantly. Tears welled up in Mathew's eyes. The boy was dead and he blamed himself for not forcing him to turn back. But his tears soon turned to anger as he remounted and continued the pursuit. He had hopes of returning later and giving the boy a proper burial. There was only one thing on his mind now and he would not rest until the murderous animals were dead.

Wolf and Reyes were now very concerned for their safety. They really believed that the two riders were probably the lead men for a posse. The chase was on and Mathew now had the advantage with a spare horse. Mathew knew that eventually the horses would begin to give out. When they did, he could then switch to a fresh mount. He also knew these two killers would ride their horses into the ground in their attempt to escape. When that happened there would be a final standoff and Mathew was ready, regardless of the outcome.

The two men managed to stay just out of rifle range for quite a while, but then the gap between them mysteriously started to close, even though the horses were still reasonably fresh. Despite the fact that Mathew had been unable to hit either man back at the oak grove, he had hit Wolf's horse. The wounded horse was now slowing down and both men were getting really worried.

By now they knew there was no posse or they were far enough behind to be no immediate threat to them. Mathew was the only one following close. That was great relief to them, but they still had to deal with the weakening horse. They would have a better chance of escape if they could just make it until dark. The wounded horse finally gave out. They stopped and Wolf got on the good horse behind Reyes. Even though they moved slower now Wolf was able to keep

Mathew at bay with an occasional rifle shot. Mathew kept his distance for his own safety and for the safety of his horses.

After some time it became obvious that Reyes's horse would not make it until dark with two riders. It was an easy decision for Wolf. He simply drew his pistol, put it to the back of Reyes's head and pulled the trigger. Reyes slumped forward and Wolf threw his body to the ground. He moved forward into the saddle and proceeded as if nothing had happened. He had planned to leave Reyes when they reached old Mexico anyway. It was just sooner, rather than later, and at least now he had a chance to elude his pursuer.

When Mathew reached the body of Reyes, he stopped to make sure he was dead. That didn't take long, since about half his face was blown away. He took the time to switch to his spare horse. The chase would be over soon and Mathew had the satisfaction of knowing there was only one man to take down now.

He mounted the fresh horse and spurred him to a gallop. He was quickly closing on Wolf now and reaching for his rifle, took his eyes off of Wolf for an instant. When he looked up Wolf was gone. He had simply disappeared in what seemed like a blink of an eye. He had to assume Wolf had gotten his horse down somehow and was waiting in ambush.

Mathew dismounted and proceeded with caution. He zigzagged as he approached the point where he had last seen Wolf. He led the horses and kept them between him and that point. Mathew heard a horse whinny but it sounded like it was crying out in pain. Mathew looked in the direction of the sound and knew then why Wolf had vanished.

There was a steep gulch just ahead of him. He moved slower now and very cautiously looked over the edge of the precipice. There below him was the horse, barely able to move his front feet as he struggled to get up. The horse was hurt very badly and not able to move his hind quarters. It was obvious the horse was going nowhere. Wolf was pinned under the horse and wasn't much better off. He had lost his rifle in the fall and was trying, unsuccessfully, to get his pistol with his left hand. His right arm, totally useless to him, was broken and bent behind and under him.

Wolf yelled, "You bastard, I think my back is broken. I can't feel my right leg. You never would have caught me if this horse hadn't tumbled and fell on me. Hell, if I had made it to dark you would have never seen me again." Mathew moved cautiously down to where the horse and Wolf lay. He took Wolf's revolver and removed a knife from his belt. "Sorry about your bad luck." Mathew said with a sneer. Wolf said, "You got lucky and now it's come to this. At least I won't strangle at the end of a rope." Wolf gave a half hearted laugh. Mathew said, "You're right about that." He went on, "I believe you're the fella that hates to burn powder. At least we agree on one thing." Mathew gritted his teeth and said, "This is for Liz and the Taylors, you son of a bitch." The shot echoed up and down the gulch. The horse was quiet now as Mathew turned to climb the steep bank and start the long journey home.

Printed in the United States
By Bookmasters